The Ballad of Booster Bogg

Ellen Jackson

Pictures by Christine Mannone Carolan

Booster Bogg
Is a rambling dog
Who wanders wild and free,

Over hill and dale

Through alleys and valleys

And down to the boundless sea.

Booster Bogg
Isn't breaking a law
As he wanders far and wide.
With a bit of luck
The dog catcher's truck
Will stop and give him a ride.

The children smile
The grown ups grin
When Bogg comes into view –
And twice a week
Collects his bone
At Baldy's Bar-B-Q.

Booster Bogg
Was once a dog
Who lived a backyard life
With Mr. Brown,
His seven kids,
And Joan, his wedded wife.

But Booster Bogg
Was a rambling dog
Whose heart could never rest,
And when the moon
Rose in the east
His voice rose in the west.

"Be quiet, Booster
Go to sleep," said Joan,
"It's half past ten."
But Booster saw
The moon and crooned
His mournful song again.

When daylight came
The family's eyes
Were bloodshot, wild and red.
They took poor Booster
To the pound
And got a bird instead.

Then Mrs. Gray
Took Booster home
And things were looking better.
She bathed him, combed him,
Clipped his nails
And knitted him a sweater.

She fed him steak
She fed him cake
He licked her little pinkie.
But Bogg got out
And rolled in something
Old with mold - and stinky!

He next belonged
To Mr. White
Who traveled every day.
So Booster Bogg
Was left alone
To jump the fence - and play.

He trespassed on
The neighbor's lawn.
"Be gone!" said Mrs. Parker.
And Booster GOT
But not before
He left a doggie marker.

"I've had enough,"
Said Mr. White.
"You take him, Mrs. Black.
Not even a wall
That's ten feet tall
Can hold this rascal back."

"Booster Bogg
Is a mighty fine dog,
On that we can agree.
I'll take him,
Mr. White, for I
Could use some company."

Now Mrs. Black
Owned just a shack
Three hens, a duck, a rooster.
There was no fence,
There was no wall
To hold a dog like Booster.

So every day
He made his way
To Panorama Park
Where he played frisbee
With the kids
Until the sky turned dark.

Sometimes he went
To meet the train
In rain or sleet or snow -
In gust or gale
He waged his tail
As if to say, "Hello."

He visited
The fire chief,
The barber and the vet.
He barked a doggie
Greeting when
The City Council met.

But someone mean
Named Mr. Green,
With squiggly, piggly eyes
Had vowed that day
The dog would pay -
He'd cut him down to size!

He rose to face
The Council saying,
"Let me read to you
A law the city
Passed in August,
Eighteen ninety-two."

"Each city dog
Must have a leash
That's made of rope or leather.
And with its owner
It must walk,
The two of them together."

The people groaned.
The Mayor moaned.
It gave them all a fright.
For Booster Bogg
Was an outlaw dog
Who didn't even bite!

Then Mr. Gold
Held up his hand.
"The fact you state is true.
But Booster Bogg
Is a mighty fine dog
And here's what we can do."

They weighed the endless
Pros and cons.
The secretary wrote.
They grumbled
And they mumbled
And at last they took a vote.

Then Mrs. Black
Took up the hat.
Each gave a small amount.
And she went out
To open up
A Booster bank account.

Now Booster has
A license, but
His leash sits on the shelf.
He's the only dog
In history
Whose owner is - himself!

He ambles here.
He rambles there.
He's freer than an eagle.
And everywhere he goes
His friends know
Booster Bogg is legal.

For Booster Bogg
Is a rambling dog
Who wanders wild and free,
Through valleys and alleys
Over hill and dale
And down to the boundless sea.

For Louise Stettinius, Bill Hopper, and Christie Hopper
because they love dogs -
E.J.

For my mother and father with love -
Christine

Library of Congress Cataloging-in-Publication Data

Jackson, Ellen B., 1943-
The ballad of Booster Bogg / Ellen Jackson; illustrated by Christine Mannone Carolan. – 1st ed.
   p. cm.
Summary: Everyone in town loves a visit from Booster Bogg – a rambling dog who became his own owner.
ISBN 978-1-934860-07-6 (hardcover : alk. paper)
[1. Stories in rhyme. 2. Dogs--Fiction.] I. Carolan, Christine, ill. II. Title.
PZ8.3.J1346Bal 2011
[E]--dc22
                    2011001674

Printed in China
first edition 1 2011
This product conforms to CPSIA 2008

Shenanigan Books
www.shenaniganbooks.com